Princess Cupcake Jones and the Queen's Closet

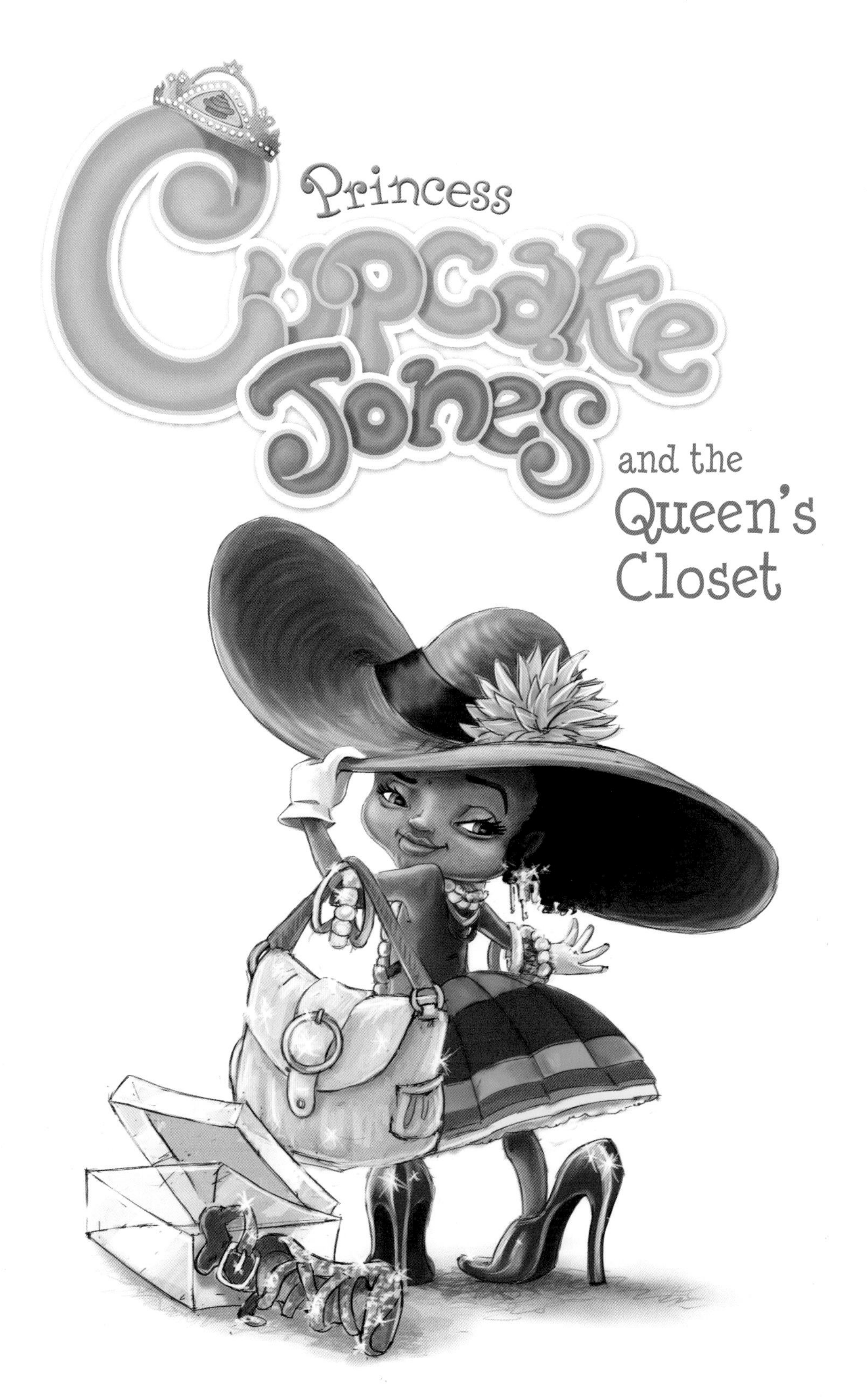

By Ylleya Fields
Illustrated by Michael LaDuca

Belle Publishing · Cleveland, Ohio

To every Cupcakette that has ever tried on their Mommy's or Daddy's shoes.
To DJ, Donna, Dakota, and Grey: Thank you for inspiring me and making life worth living. Love you!
To Stewart and Donna Kohl: Thank you for believing in me and supporting me every step of the way.
To JDE: None of this is possible without you, thanks for always pushing me to be my best.

Belle Publishing
5247 Wilson Mills Rd #324
Cleveland OH 44143
www.BellePublishing.net

Book design and illustrations by Michael LaDuca, Luminus Media LLC

ISBN: 978-0-9909986-5-5

Publisher's Cataloging-In-Publication Data
(Prepared by The Donohue Group, Inc.)

Fields, Ylleya.
Princess Cupcake Jones and the queen's closet / by Ylleya Fields ; illustrated by Michael LaDuca.

pages : color illustrations ; cm. -- ([Princess Cupcake Jones series] ; [#3])

Summary: Princess Cupcake Jones loves exploring her mom's closet and trying on shoes. In the closet, she finds herself in a transforming make-believe world of fun.
ISBN: 978-0-9909986-5-5

1. Princesses--Juvenile fiction. 2. Clothing and dress--Juvenile fiction. 3. Shoes--Juvenile fiction. 4. Imagination--Juvenile fiction. 5. Princesses--Fiction. 6. Clothing and dress--Fiction. 7. Shoes--Fiction. 8. Imagination--Fiction. 9. Stories in rhyme. I. LaDuca, Michael. II. Title. III. Title: Cupcake Jones and the queen's closet

PZ7.F545 Prq 2015
[Fic]

Printed in the USA

A castle to live in may be a child's dream,
with towers and turrets and statues that gleam.
And princesses like to sit on the thrones.
Especially Princess Cupcake Jones.

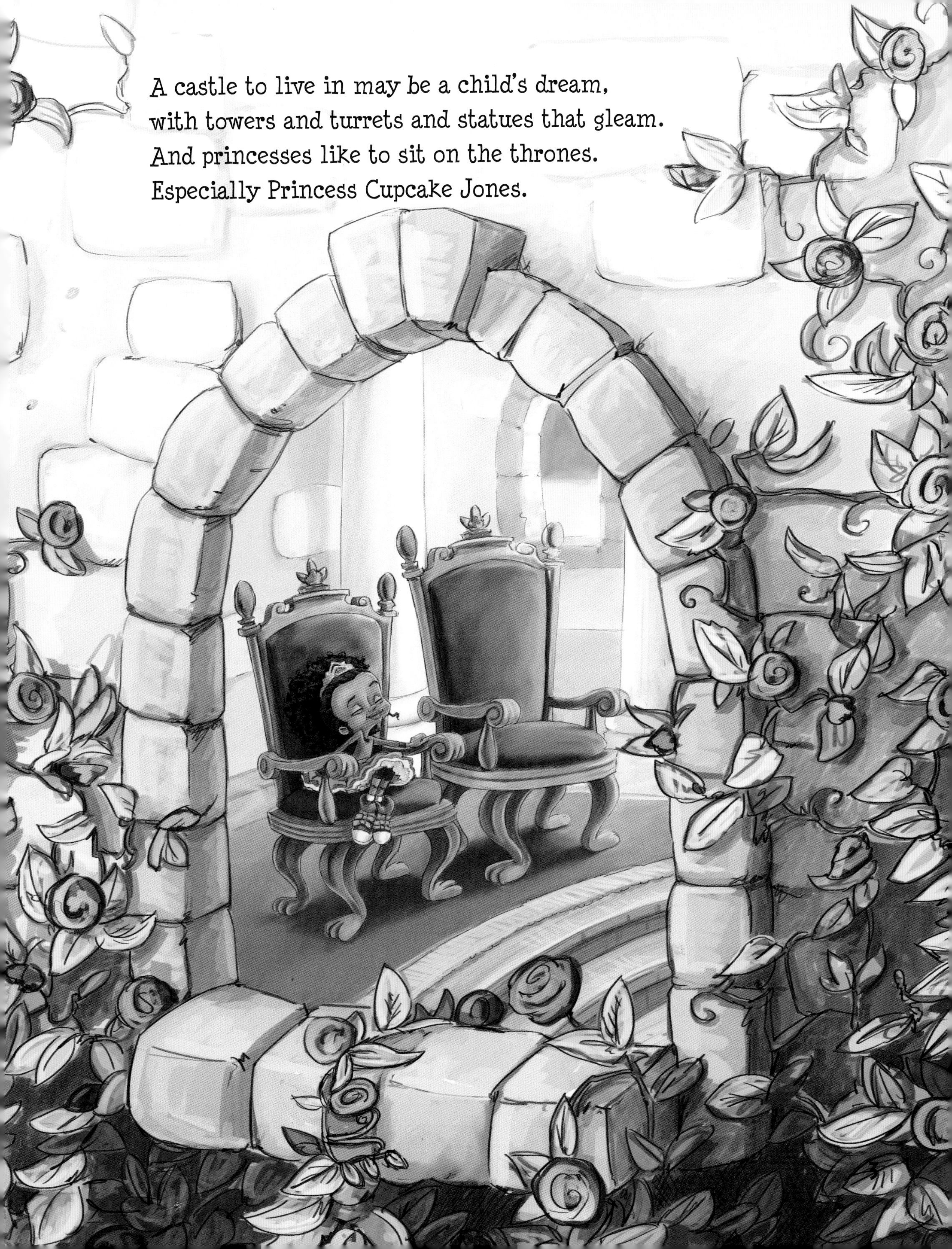

The Queen's closet was Cupcake's favorite place,
stacked high with shoes within each case.
Those shoes were amazing—the stories they told!—
a rainbow of colors from purple to gold.

Cupcake would enter the closet to play,
put on one shoe, then toss it away.
"To try on one pair would be such a bore!"
she said as she crept through the Queen's closet door.

Looking up she saw a small box out of view.
Tucked into a corner – "Is that something new?"

"I've never seen that before," Cupcake said.
"Can I reach it?" she puzzled, scratching her head.

"I know!" Cupcake yelled. "I'll climb to the top
to discover new shoes and I'm not going to stop!
I want to try on every shoe that's in here.
I'll put them all back. My Mommy won't care!"

Each shoe had a story her mother had shared.
No two of her stories could be compared.
Each tale was unique, as unique as the shoe,
so while trying shoes on, she thought of a few.

The beige flats Mom wore on the first royal date
pinched the Queen's toes and made her quite late.

The pink heels the Queen wore to the ball
made Cupcake feel almost seven feet tall.

But the very best pair had jewels in their heels
and caused Cupcake Jones to burst into squeals.
They shimmered and shined as bright as the sun,
casting patterns on walls that were hours of fun.

Shoe after shoe was tried on and then tossed.
Only one side remained, the matching side lost.

Box after box tumbled onto the floor.
With each one she grabbed, came another four more.

Higher and higher pulling shoes off each shelf,
Cupcake was feeling quite proud of herself.

Then she realized the boxes turned into a trap.
They'd fallen and scattered and plopped in her lap.
Wherever she looked, there were shoes all around.
"Oh no!" Cupcake said. "I'll never be found."

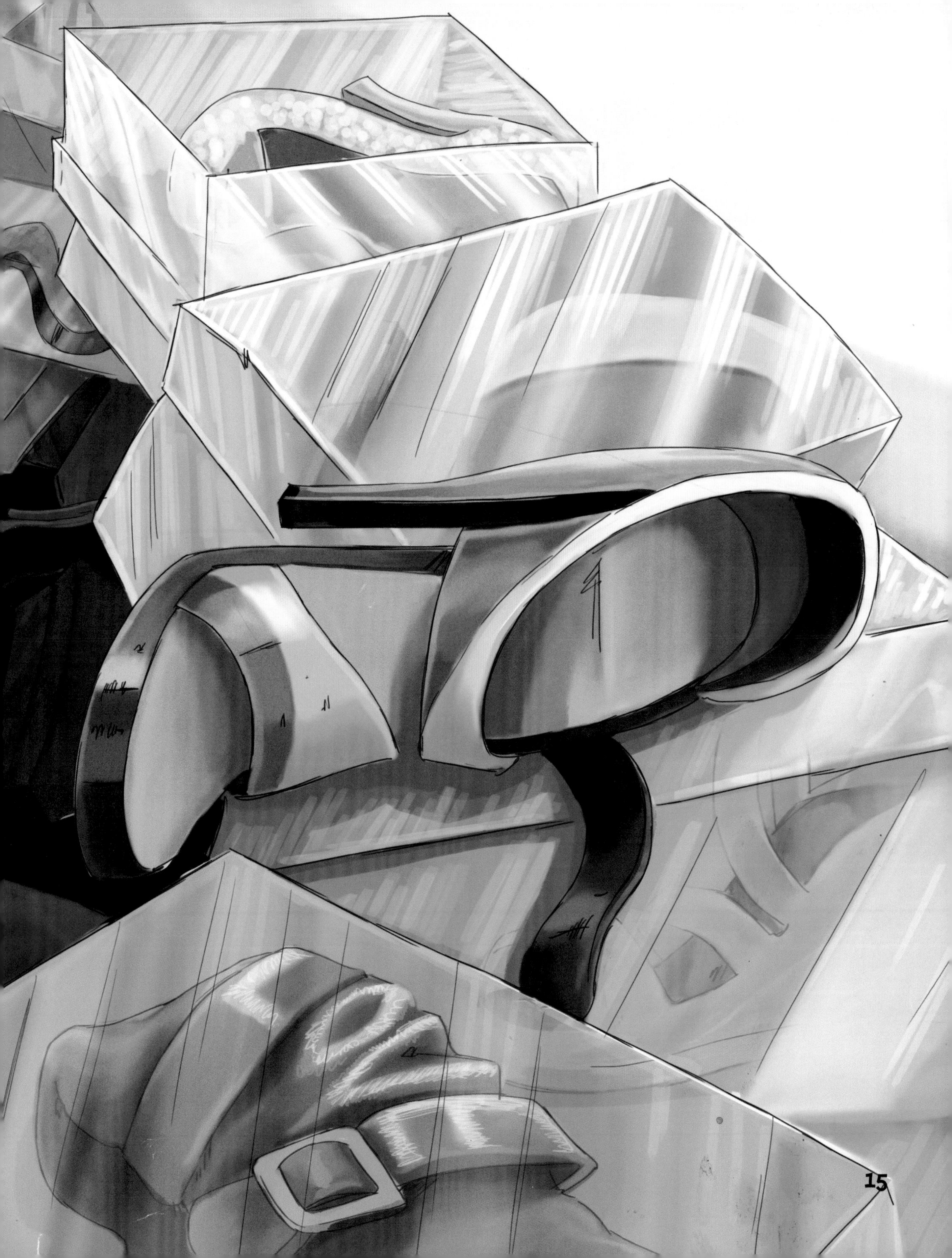

So she pushed and she pulled to climb up to the top
of the mountain of shoes that refused to stop.

Each time she climbed up, she tumbled back down.
"Help, Mommy! Help! I'm going to drown!"

In the blink of an eye, her Mommy was there.
The Queen lifted Cupcake up into the air.

"Tomorrow," Mom said, "you'll put my shoes back.
Don't worry, I'll help get them back on each rack."

As they turned from the closet and started to go,
something caught the Queen's eye and made her say, "Ohhh!"

The Queen spied the small box tucked into the pile.
She took it, she shook it, broke into a smile.

To Cupcake's surprise, it was her old Mary Janes.
They were weathered and scuffed and really quite plain.
They were her favorite when she was a baby.
Can I fit them? she thought. Maybe, just maybe.

“May I try them?” she turned to her Mommy and said.
The Queen knelt down and nodded her head.

Cupcake squeezed but only her toe would go in.
"They're too small, I think." She tapped on her chin.

"Mommy," she said. "Why'd you keep my old shoes? They don't fit anymore! I'm big, just like you."

The Queen gave a laugh. "Yes, Cupcake I know
the shoes are too small, I've watched you grow.
They are your baby shoes, this much is true,
but when I was a baby, I wore them too."

"I kept them so when you have a daughter one day,
she can wear them like we did, the very same way."

Princess Cupcake asked to be carried off to bed.
So the Queen scooped her up. “Mommy…” Cupcake said.

"When I grow up will I have as many shoes as you?"
The Queen smiled and replied, "I bet that you do!"

"Remember what's important are the memories you create,
with each shoe you wear on each special date."

With that Cupcake slept, tucked 'neath her sheet,
and dreamt dancing dreams of shoes on her feet.